The Best Kid
in the
World

To Sarah's preschool teacher, Rosie O'Connor,
and all those who welcome children to the "sweet wonderful" journey
of learning and creativity.

Atheneum Books for Young Readers

An imprint of Simon & Schuster Children's Publishing Division

1230 Avenue of the Americas

New York, New York 10020

Book design by Dan Potash

The text for this book is set in Aunt Mildred.

The illustrations for this book are rendered in ink, watercolor, gouche, and tea.

Manufactured in China

First Edition

2 4 6 8 10 9 7 5 3 1

Library of Congress Cataloging-in-Publication Data

Reynolds, Peter H., 1961–

The best kid in the world / Peter H. Reynolds.—1st ed.

p.   cm.

Summary: Jealous of her older brother's "Best Kid in the World" medal, SugarLoaf tries to figure out how to get one for herself.

ISBN-13: 978-0-689-87624-0

ISBN-10: 0-689-87624-6

[1. Brothers and sisters—Fiction. 2. Sibling rivalry—Fiction. 3. Behavior—Fiction.] I. Title.

PZ7.R33764Bes   2006

[E]—dc22   2005024032

The Best Kid in the World

A SugarLoaf Book

Written and illustrated by Peter H. Reynolds

Atheneum Books for Young Readers
NEW YORK   LONDON   TORONTO   SYDNEY

SugarLoaf *loved* birthdays,
even if it was someone else's birthday,
like her brother's.

She gave Spoke a present she had made herself.
"Extremely cool, SugarLoaf," Spoke said.
SugarLoaf clapped happily . . .

...until she saw Gramma bringing in a big box.

"Is that another present for Spoke?" SugarLoaf asked.

"No, it's his Remembering Box. You have one too," Gramma said. The box was filled with important things that Spoke had put in there each year.

Spoke pulled out a stick.

"This was my favorite toy when I was five!"
he exclaimed.

"I have a favorite boulder . . .
but it's too big to put in a box,"
SugarLoaf declared.

Then Spoke pulled out a book.

"Remember when you made that in second grade?" Dad said proudly.

I can make a book. It'll be about my boulder, SugarLoaf thought.

And then Spoke pulled out a teeny tooth in a jar.

"Ahh, your first baby tooth!" Mom sighed, beaming at him.

"I've got baby teeth too! But they're still stuck in my big-girl mouth," SugarLoaf reminded them.

Spoke peered into the box and saw another item.

It was shiny. It was sparkly. It was dazzling.

"What is it?"
Sugar Loaf asked.

"It's my Best Kid in the World Award,"
Spoke said. "Mom and Dad made it for me."

"You're the Best Kid in the World?
But . . . but . . . but what about me?"

SugarLoaf flung herself to the floor.

"Well, you won't get an award for acting like that!" Mom and Dad said.

"I won't?" SugarLoaf whimpered.

"We gave your brother that award before you were born, because he was always so helpful."

"Oh."

SugarLoaf stopped crying. She started to think.

SugarLoaf thought and thought.
She thought all night long.
She made list after list.

SugarLoaf decided the first thing she could do was to bring Gramma her favorite food. She was sleeping, so SugarLoaf left it on the table beside her.

Later she checked to see if Gramma had liked it. The ice cream was all gone, but Gramma was still asleep. Someone else had eaten all the ice cream!

SugarLoaf tried again. A basket of wash sat by the clothesline, waiting to be hung up.

I can do that, SugarLoaf thought.

She couldn't reach the clothesline, so she spread the clothes all over the yard to dry in the sun.

Later she was surprised to see
that the clothes weren't dry at all.
In fact, they were being rescued.

Dad did not look happy.

"Oh no." SugarLoaf sighed.
"I'll never win that award."

SugarLoaf decided to make her dad feel better. *Cards make people feel better*, she thought. So she made her dad a card. She slipped it under his pillow to surprise him.

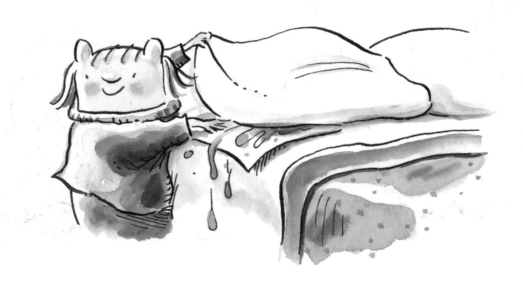

Dad was very surprised. He walked into the kitchen with his pillow covered in wet paint. SugarLoaf gasped.

She was *never* going to win the Best Kid in the World Award.

That night she tucked herself
into bed all by herself and
stared out at the moon.
Then the door opened.

Spoke was holding something. He handed it to SugarLoaf. It was shiny. It was sparkly. It was dazzling.

It was . . .

SugarLoaf's eyes grew wide. "But I messed up all day! Nothing I did counts!"

"Sugar, sweetie," said Gramma. "You tried.
All day. With a big heart. And *that's* what counts."

"Plus now we know that Floss loves
ice cream!" Spoke told her.

"And the sheets are the whitest they've ever been," added Mom.

"I've never had a more beautiful pillowcase," Dad finished.

"Now I know what I'm putting in MY Remembering Box," she cheered.

SugarLoaf celebrated with a good bounce on the bed. "Sweet wonderful!"

See you next time.